Amina's New Friends

Hi!.

Anne
O'Brien
Carelli

Copyright © 2013 by Anne O'Brien Carelli
Illustrations by Roberta Collier-Morales

Book design by The Troy Book Makers

Printed in the United States of America

The Troy Book Makers • Troy, New York • thetroybookmakers.com

To order additional copies of this title,
contact your favorite local bookstore
or visit www.tbmbooks.com

Learn more at www.aminasnewfriends.com

ISBN: 978-1-61468-165-6

Amina's New Friends

Hi! Anne O'Brien Carelli

ANNE O'BRIEN CARELLI

ILLUSTRATIONS BY ROBERTA COLLIER-MORALES

I sit still.
The woman from the Refugee Center touches my hand.

"You are a newcomer in our country, Amina," she says in Somalian.
"But you will make friends.

First they say *hi*.
Then you say *hi* back."

3

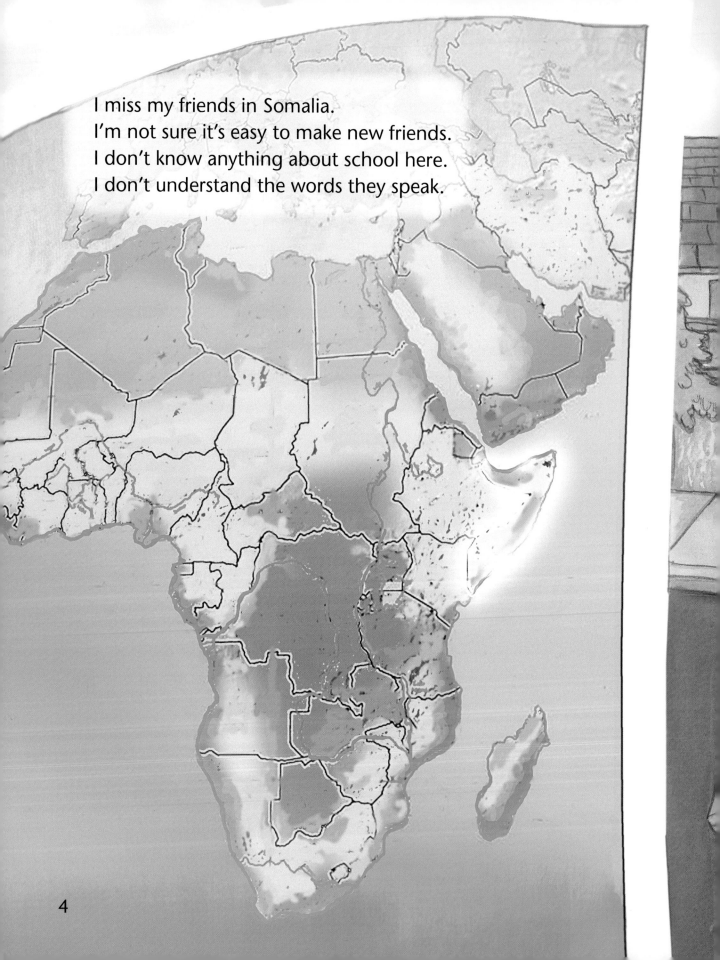

I miss my friends in Somalia.
I'm not sure it's easy to make new friends.
I don't know anything about school here.
I don't understand the words they speak.

4

Will anyone say *hi* to me?

I wait in front of my new home.
The bus comes around the corner.

I'm afraid that it's not really going to take me to school.

7

But the boys and girls on this bus are laughing.
I climb up the steps.

Some of the children look at me.
A girl moves her sweater so I can sit down.
She looks out the window.
She does not say *hi*.
Is she my friend?

The bus goes right to school.
A tall girl calls, "Amina?" She finds me in the crowd.
She leads me through long halls.
I stay close to her.

There are so many colors on the walls.
Noisy children move in all directions.
I don't want to get lost.

The tall girl stops and points to a door.
Then she walks away from me.
She waves her hand.
She never said *hi*.
Was she my friend?

My stomach feels tight.
"Come into our classroom," says a teacher.
She strokes my shoulder.

She points to my very own desk and chair.
The seat feels hard.
My knees bump against the metal desk.

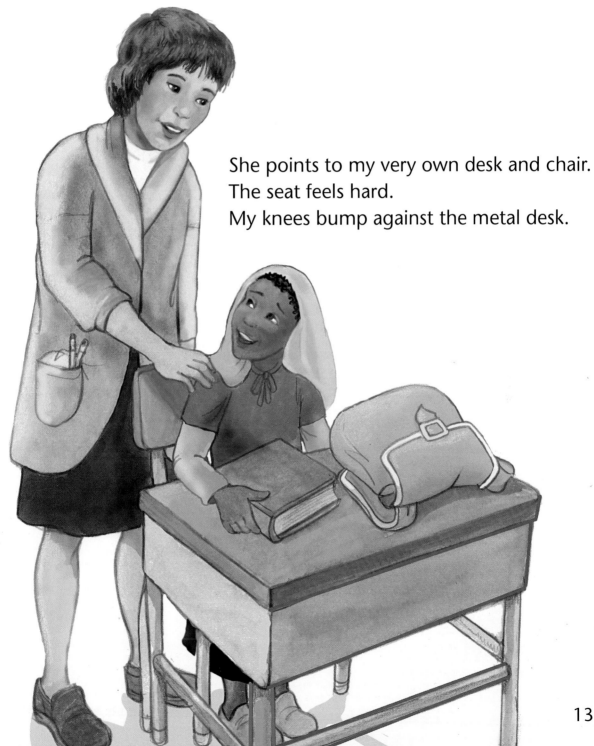

The boys and girls move their chairs so that they can see each other.
I move my chair, too.

A boy with a red shirt sits next to me.
He gives me a fat book and three beautiful sticks of color.
Does he want to be my friend?

They hold up books.
They point at pictures of animals.
A boy says, "Amina, this is a giraffe. From Africa!"
I think I understand what he says.
But I never saw a giraffe at the refugee camp.
The boy may not want to be my friend.

Suddenly the boys and girls jump up.
They stand in a line at the door.
Where are they going?
Is something wrong?
I don't want to go with them!

"Don't be scared, Amina," says a girl with a shiny necklace.
"We are going to gym."
I don't understand her.
I'm still scared.

I run with everyone on to a big green field.
A teacher blows a whistle.
She tosses a soccer ball into the air.

I know how to play!
I can kick hard and run fast!

A girl with black and yellow shoes runs up to me.
She shouts my name.
But she didn't say *hi*.
Are we friends?

The class lines up again.
Where are we going now?
This time I'm not afraid.

We enter a room that is filled with books.
A girl with a red ribbon in her hair whispers to me.

We sit at a long table.
The boys and girls turn the pages of their books.
Everyone is silent.

I can't sit quietly.
I burst out the one word that I know for sure.
Hi!

The boys and girls at my table giggle.
They all say *hi* back!
One boy says, "Shhhh…..Amina….we are in the library."

Hi! I say again.
They all laugh with me and say *hi* back.
They are my friends!

A girl with yellow hair takes me to a round table.
She shows me how to put pieces of wood together to make a big picture.
"This is a puzzle, Amina," she says.
She presses my hand to help me fit the parts together.

Then she dumps out another box of puzzle pieces.
She wants me to play with her!
She must be my friend!

We walk together to a loud room.
Everyone is eating and talking.
I scrunch up my nose at the smells.
These foods don't look like the maize and beans we ate in Somalia.
But I still feel hungry!

A girl smiles at me.
She loads my tray with full plates and bowls.
"Would you like spaghetti or a peanut butter and jelly sandwich?" she asks.
I don't know what she means.
But she's sharing food with me!
She is my friend.

We go outside again!
Some children have balls to throw.
Some jump over ropes.
Everyone is running and shouting, but they are having fun.

I sit on a swing.
I struggle to make it go high.
Hands behind me push me forward, and up I go.
We're all laughing together.
They don't say *hi* and I don't say *hi*.
But we are friends.

AUTHOR'S NOTE

It's not easy to be the new student in school. It's especially challenging if you are a refugee child.

Refugees are people who flee to escape danger in their native country. They may have been living in the middle of war, or have experienced persecution for their race, religion, social group, or political views.

It can take years to obtain permission to resettle in another country, so most refugees live in refugee camps in or near their homeland. The camps are often overcrowded and have limited food, water, and other resources. Some refugee camps have schools, but supplies can be scarce and there are few teachers for hundreds of children.

I had the wonderful opportunity to interview refugee children from all over the world who had resettled in the United States. I asked them about their experiences in American schools.

They talked about the sounds and colors and constant activity of school, and how scared they were, especially if they were just learning English.

No matter what country they were from, they said that they were most anxious about making new friends.

So please welcome all children who are newcomers facing their first day at school— and don't forget to say *Hi!*